This book belongs to:

For Tony Mitton
J.W. xx

For every Cliff who needs a Freddy in their lives -
go out there and be YOU! You are loved!
S.L.

First published in Great Britain in 2018 by Hodder and Stoughton
This edition published in 2019 by Hodder and Stoughton

Text copyright © Jeanne Willis, 2018
Illustrations copyright © Stephanie Laberis, 2018

The moral rights of the author and illustrator have been asserted.

A CIP catalogue record for this book is available from the British Library.

ISBN: 978 1 444 90824 4

1 3 5 7 9 10 8 6 4 2

Printed and bound in China

Hodder Children's Books
An imprint of Hachette Children's Group
Part of Hodder and Stoughton
Carmelite House, 50 Victoria Embankment, London, EC4Y 0DZ

An Hachette UK Company
www.hachette.co.uk

www.hachettechildrens.co.uk

FROCKODILE

BY JEANNE WILLIS

ILLUSTRATED BY STEPHANIE LABERIS

Hodder
Children's
Books

By the inky, stinky swamp where no one ever goes,
Cliff the little crocodile found a pile of clothes.

A slinky frock, stilettos and a string of pretty pearls,
and a pair of frilly underwear made for dancing girls.

He zipped himself into the frock - it fitted him just fine.

He whirled the pearls around his head and said, "I AM DIVINE!"

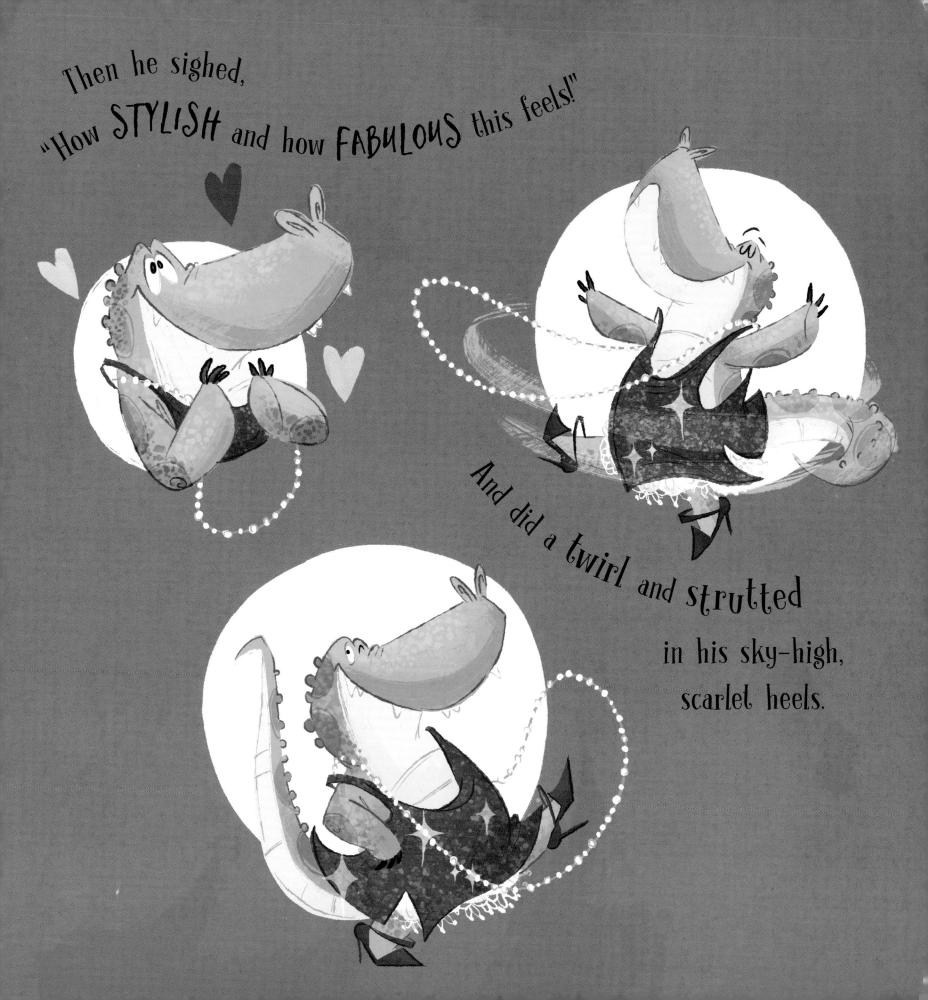

Then he sighed,
"How STYLISH and how FABULOUS this feels!"

And did a twirl and strutted

in his sky-high,
scarlet heels.

Cliff's crocodilly-daddy
was a fierce-looking guy.
A motor-biking baddy with
a patch over his eye.

No one ever challenged him
because nobody dared.
He even had the elephants
and lions running scared.

The Watering Hole

But Cliff adored his daddy, for although he looked a thug,
he always gave him bedtime kisses and a manly hug.

But would his father love him if he saw him in a frock?

Or would he be ashamed of him, or sad and die of shock?

Afraid of what his dad might say,
Cliff fell upon his knees
and begged the mean hyenas,

"Do not tell my father,
PLEASE!

I've **NEVER** dressed like this before.
Allow me to explain,
I'm just rehearsing for a play,
it's showtime once again!"

But they did not believe him
and they giggled and they jeered.

"What show? Where are the posters?
Never heard of it!" they sneered.

"It's a summer one,
this Saturday!"
Cliff fibbed in
great despair.

"Then we'll sell
tickets to our friends,"
they sniggered.
"See you there!"

Although they knew it was not true,
they ran and spread the word.

"Come to the
SPECIAL
SUMMER
SHOW!"
they said to beast and bird.

And as they told Cliff's father
of this most exciting news,
Freddy Frog found Cliff in hiding,
crying in his shoes.

"There *is* no summer play," he wept. "Perhaps I should confess.
I just feel happier in heels, and don't you **LOVE** this dress?
I want to tell my father, but I don't think I am ready."

He gathered all his froggy friends and lots of jungle folks
and swiftly wrote a summer show with songs and jolly jokes.

He gave them all a part to play and Cliff would be the star.

"Let's show the world," he said to Cliff,

"how WONDERFUL you are."

COMING SOON

FROCK
-O-
DILE

glitter, glamour
and 'gators

They rehearsed in moonlit secret, in a cave beside the sand
and Freddy hired his Uncle Charles to organise a band.

He asked his Auntie Gladys to make costumes, wigs and hats,
while the beavers built a stage
assisted by the meerkats.

Then Freddy got some glow-worms in to act as little lights
as the turtles taught the dance steps
in their tutus and their tights.

And Cliff knew all the moves
and all the words to every song...

Alas, at Friday's dress rehearsal,
all his lines were WRONG!

ACT 3

Cliff ran into the wings in tears, afraid to go on stage.
Tomorrow was the actual show! What if he lost his page?
What if his father didn't come and it was all a waste?
Or worse, what if he *did* come and it wasn't to his taste?

And what if he stopped loving him and left him in disgrace?

Freddy listened quietly and then he said to Cliff,

"My friend, why sit there worrying about 'What if? What if?'

'What is' is all that matters, and 'We are the way we are'.

You're YOU, no matter WHAT you wear and so is your Papa!"

Cliff thought about it long and hard and then he said, "I'M ME! I'll play my part with all my heart and what will be will be."

"That's the way!" said Freddy Frog and when the big day came...

Cliff stole the show! His father cheered,

"MY SON HAS SHOT TO FAME!

I'm **PROUD** of you, my boy!"
He clapped as Cliffy gave a bow.
He kissed him, then he whispered...

"May I have my pearls back now?"

And to everyone's astonishment and Cliff's delighted squeals, his dad was wearing...

FABULOUS, ADORABLE HIGH HEELS!